First published 2005 by
Brown Watson, The Old Mill,
76 Fleckney Road, Kibworth Beauchamp,
Leicestershire LE8 0HG

© 2005 Brown Watson, England

ISBN: 0-7097-1674-5

Printed in Egypt

Christmas
Stories

Brown Watson

ENGLAND

CHRISTMAS
ON THE
FARM

Illustrated by Stephen Holmes

It was a cold, wintry afternoon at Happydale Farm.

"Soon be Christmas!" said Farmer Merry. "Time to put a Christmas tree in the hall!"

"Soon be Christmas!" said his wife. "Time to cut the holly and mistletoe. I want some nice big bunches for the dining room."

"Soon be Christmas!" cried Jenny. "Time to make cotton wool snowballs to stick on the windows."
"And make lots of paper snow-flakes!" added Peter

"Moo!" went Buttercup the cow.
"Who wants cotton wool snow
and paper snowflakes? You get
REAL snow outside, where we
are, not inside, in a house!"

"But there are LOTS of things inside!" said Lenny and Lucky, the two lambs. "Just see!"

"Maybe that's because most of Christmas happens indoors," said Denny the Donkey.

The animals talked about it for a
long time. How they wished they
could go indoors, just for once!
"People talk about stars at
Christmas," said Denny. "They're
up in the sky! Look!"

As well as the stars, they saw
something else.
"It's like the sledge that Jenny
and Peter play with in the snow,"
said Denny. "A sleigh," said
Hector the Horse.

"And those are reindeer!" added Denny. "It-it's Father Christmas, the man who brings presents on Christmas Eve!"
"Couldn't we ask him to bring us something?" cried Lucky.

"We don't want presents," said Hector. "We only want to go indoors to see what Christmas is like."

"Then that's what we'll wish for!" said Denny.

"What a good idea!" said the others.

But all that happened next morning was that Mrs. Merry put a sack of straw into her car. "Come along, Jenny and Peter!" she called. "Time for school!" It seemed very odd to the animals!

The straw was for the Nativity Play which told the story of the first Christmas, when Baby Jesus was born in a stable. Jenny was going to be Mary, the mother of Jesus.

Peter and his friends, Billy and Mark, were going to be the shepherds. "Baby Jesus needs a manger to lie in," said Miss Lane, their teacher. "What could we use for that?"

"We've got a REAL manger at our farm!" Peter said proudly.

"Dad would lend it to us, wouldn't he, Mum?"

"We could bring Lenny and Lucky to school, as well," said Jenny.

But the animals were disappointed
when they heard the news.
"We ALL wanted to see Christmas
indoors!" said Lucky.
"It's not fair, just me and Lenny
getting our wish."

"Tell us all about it when you get
back!" said Hector.
"Don't forget anything!" squawked
Hetty the Hen.
"I can LOOK indoors," said Denny,
"and see for myself!"

Denny could see that Lucky and Lenny did not like being indoors. The children were kind and the play was lovely, but they felt hot and uncomfortable, and they missed their friends.

But Miss Lane was very pleased. "You have all worked hard!" she told the children as they got ready to go home. "Look, it's beginning to snow! Just in time for Christmas, too!"

It snowed all through the night. By next morning, the snow had stopped, but it was still very, very cold. All the pipes at school had frozen. Miss West said everyone had to go home.

"No Nativity Play today!" she said. "I am sorry, children."

"Oh, dear!" said Farmer Merry. "We've brought the manger and the lambs, too." But Denny the Donkey had an idea!

He ran down the lane, braying loudly. "Hee-haw! Hee-haw!" "He wants us to go back to Happydale Farm!" said Farmer Merry. "Everyone in the school mini-bus, Miss Lane!"

Buttercup the Cow, Hector the Horse and Hetty the Hen were surprised to see Denny leading the mini-bus towards the big barn at Happydale Farm. Everyone looked so excited!

"The perfect place for our Nativity Play!" cried Miss Lane. "Change into your costumes, children!" Soon, lots of people were crowding into the barn, waiting for the play to begin.

And as well as the lambs Lenny and Lucky, Denny the Donkey, Buttercup the Cow, Hetty the Hen and Hector the Horse all appeared together in the Nativity Play. What fun they had!

"So THIS is what Christmas is really about!" said Denny. "I'm glad we could share in it all."

"Well," said Hector the Horse, "that is what we wished for. Don't you remember?"

Not long afterwards, it was Christmas Eve. And as the reindeer pulled his magic sleigh across the sky, Father Christmas smiled down at all the animals on Happydale Farm.

He had brought bells for Lucky,
Lenny and Buttercup, a basket of
straw for Hetty, apples for Denny
and a blanket for Hector. How
surprised they would be on
Christmas morning!

THE TWELVE DAYS OF CHRISTMAS

On the first day of Christmas
My true love sent to me
A partridge in a pear tree.

On the second day of Christmas
My true love sent to me
Two turtle doves.

On the third day of Christmas
My true love sent to me
Three French hens.

On the fourth day of Christmas
My true love sent to me
Four calling birds.

On the fifth day of Christmas
My true love sent to me
Five gold rings.

On the sixth day of Christmas
My true love sent to me
Six geese a-laying.

On the seventh day of Christmas
My true love sent to me
Seven swans a-swimming.

On the eighth day of Christmas
My true love sent to me
Eight maids a-milking.

On the ninth day of Christmas
My true love sent to me
Nine drummers drumming.

On the tenth day of Christmas
My true love sent to me
Ten pipers piping.

On the eleventh day of Christmas
My true love sent to me
Eleven ladies dancing.

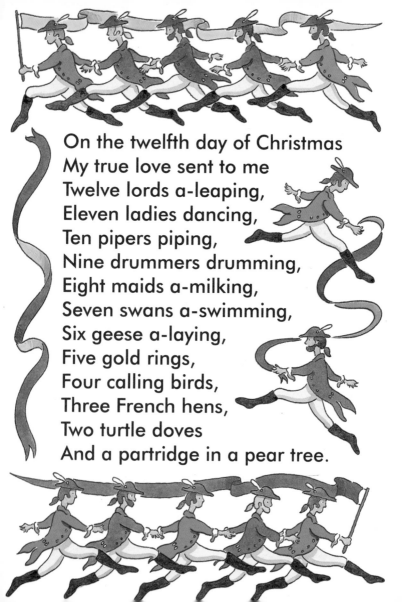

On the twelfth day of Christmas
My true love sent to me
Twelve lords a-leaping,
Eleven ladies dancing,
Ten pipers piping,
Nine drummers drumming,
Eight maids a-milking,
Seven swans a-swimming,
Six geese a-laying,
Five gold rings,
Four calling birds,
Three French hens,
Two turtle doves
And a partridge in a pear tree.

ONCE IN ROYAL DAVID'S CITY

Once in Royal David's City
Stood a lowly cattle shed,
Where a mother laid her baby
In a manger for His bed;
Mary was that mother mild,
Jesus Christ her little child.

THE NIGHT BEFORE
CHRISTMAS

'A Visit from St. Nicholas'
by Clement C. Moore

Illustrated by Colin Petty

46

'Twas the night before Christmas,
when all through the house
Not a creature was stirring,
not even a mouse;

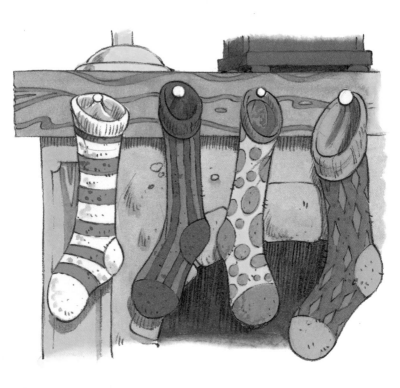

The stockings were hung
by the chimney with care,
In hopes that St. Nicholas
soon would be there.

The children were nestled
all snug in their beds,
While visions of sugarplums
danced in their heads;

And mamma in her kerchief,

and I in my cap,

Had just settled our brains

for a long winter nap;

When out on the lawn

    there arose such a clatter,

I sprang from my bed

    to see what was the matter.

Away to the window

I flew like a flash,

Tore open the shutters

and threw up the sash.

The moon, on the breast
of the new-fallen snow,
Gave a lustre of midday
to objects below,

When, what to my wondering
eyes should appear,
But a miniature sleigh
and eight tiny reindeer,

With a little old driver
    so lively and quick,
I knew in a moment
    it must be St. Nick.

More rapid than eagles,

his coursers they came,

And he whistled and shouted

and called them by name:

"Now, Dasher! Now, Dancer!

Now, Prancer and Vixen!

On Comet! On Cupid!

On Donner and Blitzen!

To the top of the porch,

to the top of the wall,

Now, dash away! Dash away!

Dash away all!"

As dry leaves that before

the wild hurricane fly,

When they meet with an obstacle,

mount to the sky,

So up to the housetop
    the coursers they flew,
With the sleigh full of toys,
    and St. Nicholas, too.

And then, in a twinkling,
I heard on the roof
The prancing and pawing
of each little hoof.
As I drew in my head,
and was turning around,
Down the chimney St. Nicholas
came with a bound.
He was dressed all in fur
from his head to his foot,
And his clothes were all tarnished
with ashes and soot;

A bundle of toys

    he had flung on his back,

And he looked like a pedlar

    just opening his pack.

His eyes – how they twinkled!

    His dimples – how merry!

His cheeks were like roses,

    his nose like a cherry.

His droll little mouth

was drawn up like a bow,

And the beard on his chin

was as white as the snow.

He had a broad face
      and a little round belly
That shook when he laughed
      like a bowlful of jelly.

He was chubby and plump,

a right jolly old elf,

And I laughed when I saw him

in spite of myself.

A wink of his eye

     and a twist of his head

Soon gave me to know

     I had nothing to dread.

He spoke not a word,

but went straight to his work,

And filled all the stockings;

then turned with a jerk,

And laying his finger

aside of his nose,

And giving a nod,

up the chimney he rose.

He sprang to his sleigh,
  to his team gave a whistle
And away they all flew
  like the down of a thistle.

But I heard him exclaim,

'ere he drove out of sight,

"Happy Christmas to all,

and to all a good night!"

JINGLE BELLS

Dashing through the snow
In a one horse open sleigh,
O'er the fields we go,
Laughing all the way;
Bells on bob-tail ring,
Making spirits bright,

What fun it is to ride and sing
A sleighing song tonight!
Jingle bells! Jingle bells!
Jingle all the way!
Oh, what fun it is to ride
In a one horse open sleigh!

SILENT NIGHT! HOLY NIGHT!

Silent night! Holy night!
All is calm, all is bright;
Round yon Virgin Mother and Child,
Holy Infant so tender and mild:
Sleep in heavenly peace,
Sleep in heavenly peace.

THE
CHRISTMAS
ELF

Illustrated by Mimi Everett

Everyone in Santa Claus' little workshop had to agree – Eddie the elf was really a very nice person. He was always smiling and cheerful – never cross or grumpy. And he was always ready to help.

"I'll carry that!" he cried when he saw Dame Jolly bringing in the teacups. "Give your arms a rest."

Poor Eddie! He didn't mean to
make Dame Jolly spill the tea!
"Oh, Eddie . . ." she sighed.
"Don't worry!" grinned Eddie –
something he often said when
things went wrong. "I'll soon wipe
it up."

"Oh dear, no!" groaned Fixit the handyman. "Not with my brand new sack!"

"Sorry!" grinned Eddie – something else he often said. "I'll wash it."

"No, wait!" cried Fixit. "There are some toy cars inside!"

SMASH! Eddie thought it was a
good idea to tip the cars out on
to the floor!
CRASH! Down fell Pink the Pixie
and Maid Merry!
"Sorry . . ." said Eddie, again.

"That's what you always say,"
groaned Fixit. "Did you remember
to take over that box of spinning
tops Santa Claus wanted?"
"Sorry!" gasped Eddie. "I forgot."

Just then, Santa Claus came in.
He did not look very pleased.
"All the paintboxes have been mixed up with the skittles!" he said. "Who packed this sack?"
"Sorry . . ." said Eddie.

"Humph! You can't carry on like
this, Eddie," grunted Santa Claus,
looking around at the mess.
"Sorry," said poor Eddie.
"I really do mean to help".

"I know, I know," said Santa Claus. "Try and help Tolly, the Teddy Bear maker, will you?" Eddie just nodded in reply. He knew he had to show that he could work well. And Tolly did need help.

"Er, just start tidying up for now," said Tolly, when Eddie asked what he could do to help.

"I've got to try and get so many Teddy Bears finished and packed up before Christmas Eve."

Kind-hearted Eddie did feel sorry for him. Suppose, he thought, just suppose he made some Teddy Bears for Tolly. Santa Claus would know what a good helper he was, then!

He was soon busy, cutting and
stitching, snipping and sewing.
The seams were a bit crooked
and one ear looked bigger than
the other, but Eddie was very
pleased with his work!

"Only the thread to cut, now," he thought. Instead, he cut a big hole in one paw! But he soon cut a patch of material to stick on top. He had just finished when Tolly gave a shout.

"Where's that piece of sparkly fur
I left here? That's all I had!"
"Oh, don't worry about that,"
said Eddie. "See what I've made."
"Th-that patch!" choked Tolly.
"It's cut from my special fur!"

"Sorry . . ." said Eddie.
"Sorry?" cried Tolly. "I've got to
finish off a batch of Teddy Bears!"
Santa Claus came in to see what
all the shouting was about, his
face was grim and unsmiling.

"I'm going to a big shop in town, tomorrow," he said at last. "You can come with me, Eddie. If you can find any child who really wants that Teddy Bear, I'll let you stay in my workshop."

Eddie the elf had never been inside a big shop, before.

The first person to come and see Santa Claus was a mummy with two children — and Eddie was sure the baby would love the Teddy Bear.

But each time he tried to give it to the baby, she kept throwing it on the floor! In the end, it got so dusty and dirty that Eddie decided to try putting it in a Christmas stocking he saw hanging on the wall.

"Here!" cried one of the shop assistants. "Who's put this old thing in our Christmas display? I'll put it out with the rubbish."
"No, wait!" shouted Eddie the elf.
"You can't do that!"

Santa Claus frowned across at Eddie. All the noise had upset a little girl and made her cry. The only thing Eddie could do now was search through the rubbish and just hope he would find the Teddy Bear . . .

And what a state the Teddy Bear was in! Dirty patches on his fur, stitches coming undone, bits of stuffing oozing out . . . who would want it, now? Eddie picked it up and went outside . . .

"Bear!" cried a little voice and a hand reached out. "Nice bear! Look, Mummy! Like Patchy!"

"No, darling," said the little girl's mummy. "It doesn't belong to you!"

"I'm sorry," the lady went on. "You see, Janey left her old rag doll on the bus last week, and it's made her so unhappy. She didn't even want the lovely, new doll Santa Claus tried to give her!"

"I thought I was the one who had made her cry," said Eddie. Janey's mummy just laughed.

"No!" she said. "You've made her smile." And Janey actually gave the Teddy Bear a big kiss!

Eddie smiled for the first time that day. And, when he said Janey could keep the bear she wanted so much, she and her mummy could not stop smiling. "Merry Christmas!" cried Eddie.

"Merry Christmas!" cried Janey. "And thank you for my present!" "Well done, Eddie," murmured Santa Claus. "Now, it's time for us to go. There's still lots of work to do before Christmas Eve!"

WE THREE KINGS OF ORIENT ARE

We three kings of Orient are,
Bearing gifts, we traverse afar-
Field and fountain,
Moor and mountain-
Following yonder star.

CHORUS:

Oh, star of wonder, star of night,
Star of royal beauty bright,
Westward leading, still proceeding,
Guide us to thy perfect light.

ALL YEAR ROUND

When Spring-time comes,
There's lots to do -
Watching birds and squirrels, too.
Flying kites and pressing flowers,
Now there are more daylight hours.

Summer-time! And, to keep cool,
We play in my big paddling pool!
Picnic lunches, games outside -
Scooters, tricycles to ride.

Autumn now, and all around,
Leaves come fluttering to the ground.
Bonfires, conkers to collect,
And the wild birds to protect.

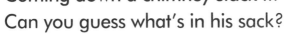

Winter comes with frost and snow,
We think of someone we all know
Coming down a chimney stack ...
Can you guess what's in his sack?

THE CHRISTMAS WISH

Illustrated by Colin Petty

114

Two men were talking outside in the
street. Dolly could hear them quite
clearly from the window sill where
she sat.

"Quite a nip in the air," said one.
"Sure sign of Christmas on the way,"
said the other. "We always look
forward to Christmas in our house!"

Dolly shivered, wishing she could pull her thin dress closer around her. If only she were still at the big house, she thought! Christmas had always been special, there...

That was when Dolly had lived in a big dolls' house, with the most delicious, warm smells wafting up from the downstairs kitchen and decorations in every room!

Once, there had even been a
Christmas tree in the big nursery.
There was a fairy doll at the very
top, smiling down at them all.
Dolly thought she was beautiful.

"If only," she thought, "if only I could wear a lovely dress like that, and hold a wand in my hand... What wishes I'd give everyone for Christmas!"

Years passed, and the little girl who owned Dolly grew up. But, somehow, Dolly was always there at Christmas. Young visitors who called often played with her.

Dolly loved every minute – until, one Christmas, she got quite a shock. "Look, Mummy!" called out one little girl. "Look at this funny, old doll!"

"It was my mother's when she was about your age," smiled her aunty. "Then she gave her to me. When I have a little girl, I expect I'll pass it on to her, too!"

There had been many little girls over the years, Dolly remembered. They all grew up – but she stayed the same. And Christmas was still her favourite time of the year.

Then, one Christmas, something happened. Underneath the big Christmas tree, there was a big parcel tied with ribbon. The little girl could hardly wait to open it!

Inside was quite the most splendid doll. She had soft curly hair, big blue eyes which opened and closed, and the loveliest dress Dolly had ever seen.

"I shall call her Arabella!" cried the little girl in delight. "Look, Mummy and Daddy! She can walk, too!"
Dolly could not help feeling sad.

The little girl played with Arabella
every day after that.

By the end of the Christmas
holidays, Dolly knew she had
been forgotten.

"What are you going to do with that old wooden doll, dear?" the little girl's Daddy asked his wife. "Is there anyone we know who would like it?"

"Not really," answered the little girl's Mummy. "Besides, children don't play with wooden dolls nowadays. She can go on the window sill for now."

And except for the times when the windows were cleaned or the window sill dusted, Dolly was quite alone. As Christmas drew near, she felt so cold, so miserable.

"Nobody would miss me here," she thought, looking out into the street. It was terrible, hearing the two men sounding so cheerful when she had never been so unhappy.

Suddenly, the door opened and the little girl's mother hurried across the room to open the window.

"Are you collecting rubbish?" she called to the two men.

"Can you take a pile of old newspapers?"

"Be right with you, ma'am!" one shouted back. They didn't see Dolly falling out into the street!

She lay there for what seemed a very long time, cold and wet and wishing she could cry for help.
Every so often, she would hear somebody talking about Christmas.

"Hello!" cried a voice, and Dolly felt a rough hand picking her up. "What have we got here?"
"Something for the rubbish tip, I reckon, Mike!" said someone else.

Fear made Dolly feel colder than ever. Then the first man said, "Oh, I might as well take her home. Maybe my little girl will like her." Dolly did hope so!

"Well," said the man when he
showed Dolly to his daughter.
"What do you think?"
"Why can't she move her arms
and legs?" asked the little girl.

"Because she's made of wood, silly!" laughed the little girl's mother. "Your Nana had one just like this when I was about your age. She was fun to play with!"

"And," her mummy went on, "she's just what we need for Christmas!" Soon, the little girl was wiping all the mud and dirt off Dolly. And, as for her mummy…

She made Dolly a pretty fairy dress
with silver wings, a tinsel crown
and a lovely, silver wand. Dolly
was ready to grant all the wishes
made around the Christmas tree!

"I wonder if Dolly gets a wish,
too?" said the little girl.
"You know," said her mummy, "I
think she's had her wish already!"
"And so I have," thought Dolly.

MY SNOWMAN FRIEND

I call him Mr. Frosty-Face!
He brings us so much fun,
He has coal eyes, a carrot nose
And a smile for everyone!

When I talk, I know he'll listen
To every word I say,
I can shout, or knock his hat off,
And he'll never run away!

But when the weather's warmer,
Then Frosty-Face must go –
Until the next time that he comes
With winter's ice and snow.

GOOD KING WENCESLAS

Good King Wenceslas looked out,
On the feast of Stephen,
When the snow lay round about,
Deep, and crisp, and even:

Brightly shone the moon that night,
Though the frost was cruel,
When a poor man came in sight,
Gath'ring winter fuel.

SANTA'S
LITTLE HELPER

Illustrated by Colin Petty

It was always cold where Peter lived – almost as cold as the land where Santa Claus came from. And with all the ice and snow and the green fir trees reaching up to the sky, everywhere always looked Christmassy, too – especially when Peter and his dad came back from town on the sledge!

The sledge was always loaded up when Christmas was coming. Not with toys and presents, but with food, clothes and everything else Peter's family needed. A team of dogs pulled it across the snow.

Peter loved all the dogs and helped to look after each one. His favourite was Marcus, the leader. "Daddy," Peter said one day, "why does Santa Claus have reindeer to pull his sleigh?"

"I suppose because he's always had reindeer," smiled Daddy. "I just happen to like dogs best." "So do I!" said Peter. "Marcus could pull the sleigh across the sky without any trouble."

Peter went indoors to write his Christmas letter. What he wanted more than anything else was a guitar. "My Daddy could teach me how to play it," he wrote, "and everyone would enjoy the music."

Peter finished by writing about his clever dog, Marcus. But he was wondering if Father Christmas really could bring the guitar he wanted so badly. He had only ever seen a picture of one, in a book.

An icy blast of wind lifted Peter's letter up and up into the dark, wintry sky, until it was like a big snowflake, whirling round and round. Then, at last, it floated down on a cloud.

At least, it looked like a cloud to anyone who might have been watching. But really, it was a heap of letters. "We'll never get all these sorted out!" someone cried. "It's Christmas Eve, soon!"

"We'll manage!" came a jolly-sounding voice – and a big chubby hand in a red sleeve picked up Peter's letter. "How many times have I said that Christmas comes but once a year?"

But even Santa Claus had to admit that he and his workshops did seem to be extra busy! There was so much to do! Toys to be sorted out, presents wrapped and loaded on to his sleigh . . . .

"Mind out, Prancer!" puffed Santa
Claus, helping to drag a big sack
of toys across the snow. "Ooh, I'll
be glad to get this lot on the
sleigh. Then I think we'll have a
nice cup of tea . . . ."

Poor Santa! His hands were so cold that the edge of the sack slipped from his fingers.
Teddy Bears, footballs, cars, games . . . . out they all tumbled, rolling around on the snow!

Poor Prancer! He stepped back on a big, toy engine – and down he went, too!

"Prancer!" cried Santa Claus in alarm. "Prancer, are you all right?"

"No Christmas Eve duties for you, boy!" said Santa Claus seeing his hurt leg. Prancer was very upset. And Santa knew the other reindeer could not pull a heavy sleigh without him . . . .

All was quiet that Christmas Eve. Everyone had been working hard. Now all that could be heard was the rustle of coal as it shifted on the fire and the whisper of snow against the window.

Peter was fast asleep, dreaming of everyone singing and dancing to his guitar, just as he had told Santa Claus. He did not hear a low whistle outside in the snow. But someone else did . . . .

"Here, Marcus, old boy!" called Santa Claus, as the dog appeared. "Peter told me all about you. Would you like to help pull my sleigh?" Marcus wagged his tail without stopping.

Santa Claus put on the jangly harness, just like Peter fastened the straps when Marcus pulled the sledge. But, as soon as he stepped out with the reindeer – can you guess what happened?

The sleigh lifted up into the sky, stars twinkling all around!
"Get some speed up!" cried Santa Claus, shaking the reins with a merry, jingling sound. "Lots to do before Christmas morning!"

And so there was. Hundreds of chimney stacks, thousands of roofs, across towns and big cities, farms and villages! Santa Claus and his sleigh visited them all. Marcus had never seen such sights!

Dawn was just beginning to break
as Santa Claus steered the sleigh
back to Peter's home. "Thanks for
your help, Marcus!" he said,
giving him a pat. "We'd never
have managed without you!"

Peter got up early next morning. "Do you know," he said sleepily, "I had a lovely dream last night. It was all about Marcus going with Santa Claus, helping the reindeer to pull his sleigh!"

"You were asking me if I thought Marcus could do the job," Daddy smiled. "So maybe you went to bed wondering about it. Anyway, come and see what Santa Claus has left for you."

There were sweets, toys – and a big parcel with a label tied on it. "DEAR PETER," it read, "HERE IS A SPECIAL PRESENT FOR TELLING ME ABOUT YOUR DOG, MARCUS. HE WAS A GREAT HELP TO ME AND MY REINDEER!"
Peter did not know which he

liked best – the note from Santa
Claus, or the lovely guitar!
And Marcus? He settled down for
a nap. Pulling a heavy sleigh all
night long had been hard work!

AWAY IN A MANGER

Away in a manger,
No crib for a bed,
The little Lord Jesus
Laid down His sweet head;

The stars in the bright sky
Look down where He lay,
The little Lord Jesus
Asleep on the hay.

TEDDY'S FAVOURITES

What does a Teddy Bear like best?
Perhaps you'd like to know!
Well...swings and whirly roundabouts
And a bouncy ball to throw...

Currant buns and chocolate,
Honey spread on bread,
And listening to a story,
When I'm tucked up in bed.

Sandcastles! Iced lollipops!
A friendly dog or cat!
Listening to the rain outside
As it goes pitter-pat...

Fireside chats when winter comes...
A gift from Santa Claus...
I think that's all my favourite things.
Can you tell me some of yours?

THE
CHRISTMAS
SNOWMAN

Illustrated by Colin Petty

"It's cold enough for snow!" said Simon and Julie's dad, as he took one last look out at their back garden. Then he locked the door for the night.

"I hope not!" said Mum, who was busy baking Christmas cake and mince pies. I really hate going Christmas shopping when it's snowy and cold."

All the same, Simon and Julie couldn't help wishing that it WOULD snow – even if it was just enough to build a snowman for Christmas! And when they woke up next day – what do you think?

184

Roofs of houses and garden sheds, window sills and fences were powdered with snow, sparkling in the winter sunshine like icing sugar. "Great!" Simon cried. "We can build a snowman."

"You'll have to be quick!" laughed
Dad. "We didn't have much snow,
and it won't last long."

"Good!" said Mum, mixing the
cake. "I'm glad," added Gran.

The children put on their coats, wellingtons, woolly hats and gloves and went outside. "It's true what Dad says," sighed Julie looking around. "There isn't really all that much snow . . ."

"I think there's enough by the wall," Simon told her, scooping up quite a few handfuls. "See if you can make a big snowball for the head, and I'll start on the snowman's body."

Julie found that getting enough snow even to make a little snowball was not easy. Scraping the whole of the garden fence only gave her a tiny handful, and most of that was already melting.

Simon had not done much better with the snowman's body. And if Mum hadn't opened an upstairs window, sending down a shower of snow, they would not have managed to finish him, at all.

"He's a bit small . . ." said Julie.
"Don't worry!" said Simon. "We
can always make him bigger, as
long as we get some more snow
before Christmas. Let's call him
Snowy, the Christmas Snowman!"

The weather stayed quite cold,
but there was no more snow.
"At least I can hang out some
washing," said Mum.
"And I can do some Christmas
shopping," smiled Gran.

Julie and Simon were very disappointed.

"Oh, don't worry about your snowman," Dad told them. "That wall gets hardly any sun, you know. He'll last until Christmas."

But there was no mistake about it. Snowy was getting smaller and smaller. And the smaller he got, the easier it became for the pale, winter sun to melt more and more of him away.

If it had not been for Jack Frost coming round every night and touching everything with his long, icy fingers, Snowy knew he would never have lasted so long.

Everyone else seemed so happy. Fairy lights appeared in all the windows. Snowy could hear Julie and Simon laughing and chatting as they helped to put up the decorations.

"Time to mix the Christmas pudding!" came Mum's voice. "Take it in turns to make a wish!" "I'd wish to be a real Christmas snowman!" thought Snowy.

Snowy glanced up at the dark sky, hoping he'd see clouds gathering around him, hiding the moon before the first snowflakes drifted down. Instead, it was a clear night, with lots of stars.

He looked again. Something was gliding towards the moon, something piled high, with a man in boots and a hood, pulled by animals with what looked like tree branches on their heads . . .

"Reindeer . . ." whispered Snowy.
Simon and Julie had talked a lot
about Santa Claus and what they
hoped he would bring them on
his sleigh. Snowy knew he came
from a land of ice and snow . . .

"I wish Santa Claus could bring me some snow," thought poor Snowy. He closed his eyes tight, not wanting to see anything to remind him of the happy time Christmas was meant to be.

At first, Snowy thought he was

dreaming. Something soft began
falling on his face, his head, then
his body. It fluttered all around
him like a shower of bright
moonbeams, making him feel
warm and happy . . .

"Snow!" cried Snowy joyfully.
"Merry Christmas!" came the cry from above. "Merry Christmas, Snowy!" And in a final burst of stars and moonbeams, both reindeer and sleigh were gone.

203

"Well, I got just what I wanted for Christmas," said Dad in his new dressing gown. "So did we!" cried Julie and Simon. "Except for our Christmas snowman," added Julie solemnly.

"Well," said Grandma, standing at the back door. "I don't know about that. See for yourselves, you two!" Simon and Julie looked at each other, sure that there had been no snow at all.

Snowy, the Christmas snowman stood proud and tall. His head was round and jolly, and his body so plump and cuddly that Julie could not help giving him a hug for Christmas morning.

"Where did all the snow come from?" they wondered. "And why isn't there snow anywhere else?" When Julie said that it might have something to do with Santa Claus, how they all laughed!

POOR OLD SANTA

We've put up the decorations
With plenty of holly to see,
We've helped Mummy to make
Mince pies and a cake,
We've got the star for our tree!

We've hung our Christmas stockings,
But the chimney we did not clean!
Now, there's soot, dirt and mess,
Santa's stuck there unless . . .
He can wait 'til the chimney
sweep's been!

SANTA'S SLEIGH

Have you ever wondered
Where Santa leaves his sleigh,
When he brings toys for children
To find on Christmas Day?

For reindeers, all the roof-tops
Are much too smooth and steep!
One slip, they'd go sliding down,
And land in one big heap!

But if they were in the garden,
How could Santa with his sack,
Climb right up to the roof-top,
Then down the chimney stack?

There's so much danger in the road,
So, where CAN he leave his sleigh?
Perhaps you'd like to ask him,
When he comes round your way!

SANTA'S
BUSY DAY

Illustrated by Stephen Holmes

Santa had been very busy all morning, getting ready for Christmas Eve!

"Have a rest, Santa!" cried an elf. "You're always so busy!"

"But I LIKE being busy!" said Santa. "And do you know the job I like best of all?"

"Riding the sleigh!" said the elf.
"Putting all the toys in sacks!"
cried the Christmas Fairy.
"Wrong!" laughed Santa.
"What I like best is reading all
my letters."

"Your letters!" cried the little Christmas elf. "That reminds me! Has anyone written asking for a little wooden engine, Santa? This one gets left behind every Christmas Eve."

"I don't think so..." said Santa. "Can you put it in my sack? I really MUST read these letters. They're from children in the town I'm visiting tomorrow!" Suddenly, he stopped.

"Listen to this!" he said.
"Dear Santa, will you please bring an extra nice present as a Christmas surprise for our daddy. Thank you. Lots of love from Tina and Tom!"

"If only Tina and Tom had said what they wanted for their daddy!" groaned Santa. "How do I know what he would like?" "What about some hankies?" said the Christmas Fairy.

"That doesn't sound much of a surprise!" said Santa. Then Penny Pixie, who helped look after the reindeer, had an idea.
"What about one of your Christmas beakers?" she said.

Santa Claus gave a big smile. "Now that's a REAL Christmas surprise!" he said.
"I can't wait to see Tina and Tom's faces when I meet their daddy tomorrow!"

Very early the next morning,
Santa got ready to begin his long
journey. "Wrap up warmly!" said
Penny, tucking a scarf inside his
cloak. "You're sure to have a very
busy day!"

It was still dark when the town where Tina and Tom lived came in sight. "Put me down beside that big Christmas tree," Santa told the reindeer, "and then you can take the sleigh back home!"

Soon, Santa knew, he would be busy meeting people and hearing what everyone wanted for Christmas! He was looking forward to seeing Tom and Tina with their daddy.

He didn't have long to wait.
"Look, Daddy!" someone cried,
and a girl and a boy came
hurrying up. "Tina and Tom!"
smiled Santa. "Here's that
Christmas surprise for Daddy!"

"We're Mike and Mandy, not Tina and Tom!" said the boy. "And I'm Paddy, their big brother!" said the man. "But thanks for the surprise, Santa! It's just what I've always wanted!"

"Oh, no!" thought poor Santa. "What can I give Tina and Tom's daddy, now?" Just then, up came another boy and girl, with someone wearing a crash helmet and motorbike leggings.

"Come on Tom!" cried the girl.
"Tom!" thought Santa. "Tom and
Tina with their daddy!" Without
thinking, he unwound the scarf
from inside his cloak and handed
it across.

"Here's a Christmas surprise for you, sir!" he cried. "A very merry Christmas!" Tom gave a cheer. "Just what Sam wanted!" he cried. "She looks after us."
"Sam?" echoed Santa Claus.

The person took off the crash helmet with a shake of her long, fair hair. "A scarf!" she cried. "Just the thing when I'm riding my motorbike, eh, kids?" And Sam gave Santa a big kiss!

So many people wanted to see
Santa Claus on that busy day!
Everyone looked so pleased and
so happy, he could not help
smiling. But at the same time, he
was also very worried.

Santa had been so busy, giving out lots of lovely things from his sack, that soon there would be nothing left at all!

"Oh dear!" thought poor Santa Claus. "Whatever shall I do?"

"Hello, Santa!" someone said, and Santa Claus turned to see a girl in a bobble hat. "I'm Tina and this is my brother, Tom! Did you get our letter about a surprise for our daddy?"

"Er, well..." Santa stopped, and without thinking, he put his hand deep into his sack, feeling around at the very bottom. There was something small and hard, tucked away in one corner.

It was the little wooden engine!
Tom and Tina's daddy gave a big
smile, reaching out to touch it.
"A model engine!" he cried. "I've
always wanted a model engine!
Thank you, Santa!"

"You ARE clever, Santa!" said
Tina. "Tom SAID you'd know what
Daddy wanted!" Tom looked very
proud. And their daddy? He just
kept looking at the little wooden
engine!

Santa was chuckling all the way
home! "Why did I worry about
that Christmas surprise?" he kept
saying. "I only had to remember
that grown-ups never quite stop
being children!"

It was soon dark. Snow began
falling and Santa was glad to see
the lights from his workshop.
"I'll be glad to have a rest!" he
told his reindeer. "I've had SUCH
a busy day!"

THE HOLLY AND THE IVY

The holly and the ivy,
When they are both full grown,
Of all the trees that are in the wood,
The holly bears the crown.

CHORUS:
The rising of the sun
And the running of the deer,
The playing of the merry organ,
Sweet singing in the choir.

The holly bears a berry,
As red as any blood,
And Mary bore sweet Jesus Christ
To do poor sinners good.

The holly bears a prickle,
As sharp as any thorn,
And Mary bore sweet Jesus Christ
On Christmas Day in the morn.

The holly bears a bark,
As bitter as any gall,
And Mary bore sweet Jesus Christ
For to redeem us all.

I SAW THREE SHIPS

I saw three ships come sailing in,
On Christmas Day, on Christmas Day,
I saw three ships come sailing in,
On Christmas Day in the morning.

And what was in those ships all three?
On Christmas Day, on Christmas Day,
And what was in those ships all three?
On Christmas Day in the morning.

Our Lord Jesus Christ and his lady,
On Christmas Day, on Christmas Day,
Our Lord Jesus Christ and his lady,
On Christmas Day in the morning.

THE LITTLE
CHRISTMAS
TREE

Illustrated by Stephen Holmes

ONCE, on a hill above a town, there was a little Christmas tree. So many big trees grew all around, there was no room for the little tree to spread its roots, so it hardly grew at all. Nobody even knew that the tiny little Christmas tree was even there.

As Christmas time drew near, the little tree always felt so unhappy. He could see people looking at all the other trees and hear the children laughing and talking to each other.

"Ooh, look at that lovely big Christmas tree!"

"We can hang lots of presents on those strong branches!"

"This Christmas tree is so nice and tall!"

"Choose me!" thought the little Christmas tree. "Please choose me!" But nobody did. Then, one cold winter's night, something happened. Quite suddenly, a strong wind began to blow.

The wind howled down all the chimneys, blew under all the doors and rattled all the windows. And it whistled through the branches of all the trees, tugging hard at the roots.

The little Christmas tree held on for as long as he could. But then a sudden gust of wind blew hard against the bottom branches and he felt himself being lifted high into the air!

"Whoo-Whoo!" whistled the wind, blowing harder than ever. Only one person saw the little Christmas tree whirling and twirling about on that cold, snowy night.

Gradually, the wind died down, as more big, white snowflakes fell from the sky. The little Christmas tree felt himself falling, falling, until he came to rest on a bed of snow.

"About time, too!" came a voice, and a figure in a red cloak and big boots picked up the little Christmas tree. "You always wanted to be a proper Christmas tree, didn't you?"

Little by little, the sky became
lighter and a pale sun shone
down. "Hey, here's the Christmas
tree we wanted!" someone
shouted. "Mum said Santa would
bring it, Jason!"

"Let's take it indoors," came a boy's voice, "then we'll find a big flower pot or something and fill it with earth. We'll soon have this looking like a real Christmas tree!"

"I'm glad it's a little Christmas tree!" said Anna. "Big trees need lots of decorations!"
"And it's tall enough for me to reach the top branch!" laughed Jason. "I like it!"

They worked hard all morning, cutting out paper stars, making balls of silver foil and hanging things on all the branches. The little Christmas tree loved every minute!

There were lots of games and parties and fun around the little Christmas tree! Someone caught their sleeve on a branch and a small piece broke off. The little Christmas tree tried not to mind.

"Our poor tree!" said Anna.
"All its little green needles are beginning to fall off."
"That always happens," said someone else. "Christmas trees don't last long indoors!"

By the time Christmas was over, the little Christmas tree was very worried. "We'll put the decorations in the cupboard ready for next year!" said Mum. "Any rubbish for the dustmen?"

"What about the little Christmas tree?" asked Jason. "We can't put that in the cupboard."

"No," said Mum, lifting the Christmas tree out of its flower pot. "It will have to go outside."

The poor little Christmas tree trembled so much that a whole shower of green needles fell to the ground. He was taken outside and set down by a cold wall, waiting for the dustmen.

After a while, the little tree was
lifted up again – but he hardly
cared. All he had ever wanted
was to be a real Christmas tree.
He had never been so unhappy.

He began to dream that he could hear birds singing, just as they did when he had been with the other trees on the hillside. He thought he heard a voice which sounded just like Jason.

"Look at the birds! They're eating all the food we've put round our tree!" The little Christmas tree looked down at his new, green branches, with the birds darting in and out.

"That little tree has certainly brightened up our back yard!" said Mum.

"YOU always said nothing would grow, because we don't get much sunshine!" said Jason.

"But we really don't WANT our Christmas tree to grow!" said Anna. And all through the months that followed, the birds would come and perch on the tree, chirping and singing.

As the days grew shorter, the time came for the birds to fly away to warmer lands. But the little Christmas tree did not mind. Soon, he knew, winter would come once again.

Then he would be a real little
Christmas tree again, with stars
and silver balls. Anna and Jason
loved him. "Because," said Jason,
"we can have a little bit of
Christmas all year round!"

WE WISH YOU
A MERRY CHRISTMAS

We wish you a Merry Christmas,
We wish you a Merry Christmas,
We wish you a Merry Christmas
And a Happy New Year!

O CHRISTMAS TREE!

O Christmas Tree! O Christmas Tree!
Thy leaves are so unchanging:
Not only green when summer's here
But also when 'tis cold and drear.
O Christmas Tree! O Christmas Tree!
Thy leaves are so unchanging.

THE CHRISTMAS FAIRY

I am the Christmas fairy –
And everything I see,
With wand and crown,
As I look down
From the top branch of the tree!

I see the pretty coloured lights,
The cards hung on the wall,
Candies and sweets,
And Christmas-time treats
For visitors when they call.

What fun on Christmas morning!
I'll remember all I saw,
When I'm put away
Until the day
I'm on the tree, once more.

TEDDY'S
CHRISTMAS
PRESENT

Illustrated by Andrew Geeson

Teddy Bear had lots of nice toys. He had building bricks, a drum, a scooter, and lots of books and crayons. But his favourite had always been Ernest the Engine. Teddy loved his big, smiley face and the clickety-clack, clickety-clack of his wheels, as he pulled the train behind him.

Ernest had been Teddy's friend
ever since he could remember.
But now, the old engine was
becoming very battered and
worn. More than once, a wheel
had come off and Daddy Bear
had fixed it back on.

His face had become cracked, his buffer beam was bent and his paintwork was scratched. And more than once, his funnel had come off! "I don't know how many more times I can mend Ernest," said Daddy.

"Ernest is getting quite old now, you know," Daddy Bear went on, reaching for his screwdriver. "And you play with him every day, Teddy." "I know," said Teddy sadly. He wondered what he could do.

Just then, Mummy Bear came in,
a shopping basket over her arm.
"What do you think?" she cried.
"Santa Claus is coming to Teddy
Town tomorrow, to see what all
the teddies want for Christmas!"

"Hear that, Teddy?" smiled Daddy. "You can ask him to bring you a nice, new engine! You've been a good bear all year, so I think Santa Claus would do it."
But Teddy Bear shook his head.

"No," he said, "I don't want a new engine to take the place of Ernest, just because he's old and tired." Then, he thought again. "But I could ask Santa Claus to make him as good as new, couldn't I?"

He sat down to write to Santa Claus that same afternoon, telling him all about Ernest. "I do not want any new toys," he wrote, "but I hope you can make Ernest like new. Please try. Love Teddy."

Santa Claus did not see how he could help. "Toys do get old," he said, stroking his beard. "It's a pity Teddy does not want a new engine. Eric's a nice little one, and he needs a good home . . ."

"All the same," Santa thought, "I know how Teddy feels. I only wish I could make old toys into new ones." A sudden movement of snow caught his eye and he looked across towards the stables.

Dasher had been away having his hooves trimmed, all ready for Christmas Eve. Now, he was back with Dancer, and seeing how glad both reindeer were to be together gave Santa Claus an idea!

The teddies of Teddy Town were pleased to see Santa Claus sitting by the big Christmas tree in the market. He soon saw Teddy Bear coming towards him, holding Ernest the engine very tightly.

"So, this is Ernest," he said, in a voice which made Ernest feel very proud. "Yes, I can see why you love him so much, Teddy."

"Can you make him like new again?" asked Teddy.

"Well," said Santa Claus, "I can't make him a new engine on the outside, but I think I can make him a new engine inside. Would that do?" Teddy did not really understand this, but he nodded and smiled.

"As long as I don't have a new engine in place of Ernest," he said. "No, Teddy," Santa Claus laughed, reaching in his sack. "But I do have something so that Ernest will be able to rest a little."

It was a lovely, little engine shed!
Teddy could hardly wait to take it
home and see what Ernest looked
like, resting inside.
"Oh, thank you, Santa Claus!" he
cried. "Thank you very much!"

Teddy put the shed on the floor and backed Ernest inside.

"There you are, Ernest!" he smiled. "You have a nice rest, just like Santa Claus said. You'll soon start feeling like new."

But, after a while, Teddy became bored just looking at Ernest in the shed. He was sure, too, that the trucks wanted to go round on the rails – if only they had an engine to pull them along!

Teddy felt rather muddled. He did think that Santa Claus had given him a special, magic sort of present to make Ernest feel like new again. Yet, nothing had happened.

But, Teddy was wrong. Being alone in the engine shed had made Ernest think how nice it would be to have a friend. So, he was very pleased when someone in a red cloak and hood put another engine beside him!

"Hello," whispered the new, little
engine with a friendly grin.
"My name is Eric!"
"And I'm Ernest!" whispered Ernest.
"Merry Christmas to you, engines!"
whispered Santa Claus.

Ernest and Eric talked long into the night, chatting about trains and tracks. It made Ernest feel most important, telling his new friend all about Teddy Bear and the fun they would share.

And what a surprise Teddy had on Christmas morning! It was hard not to like such a bright, cheerful-looking engine, such as Eric – especially when Teddy could see he was already Ernest's friend!

And Ernest? Well, his funnel was still wobbly and his wheels loose, but his smile was bright and his paintwork sparkled. It was plain he felt a new engine inside, just as Santa Claus had promised!

And, as Ernest watched Eric
pulling the trucks, Teddy could see
that he did not mind having a
rest. And how much nicer the
shed looked with two engines to
go inside! Clever old Santa Claus!

GOD REST YE MERRY GENTLEMEN

God rest ye merry gentlemen:
Let nothing you dismay.
Remember, Christ our Saviour
Was born on Christmas Day,
To save us all from Satan's power
When we were gone astray.

CHORUS:

Oh, tidings of comfort and joy,
Comfort and joy,
Oh, tidings of comfort and joy!

OH COME, ALL YE FAITHFUL

Oh come, all ye faithful,
Joyful and triumphant,
Oh come ye,
Oh come ye to Bethlehem.
Come and behold Him,
Born the King of Angels

CHORUS:

Oh come, let us adore Him,
Oh come, let us adore Him,
Oh come, let us adore Him,
Christ the Lord!

THE MAGIC REINDEER

Illustrated by Stephen Holmes

Ronnie the reindeer was always in trouble! "Oh, Ronnie!" cried Mother Deer. "How DID you get your antlers tangled up in this holly bush?"

"RONNIE!" roared Stag. "Why MUST you charge through the stream and splash water about? Look, I'm dripping wet!"

But as soon as Ronnie saw a bird in the sky or leaves rustling on a bush, off he'd dash. Then it would be, "Ronnie! Don't tread in our water!" or "Ronnie! You've splashed us with mud!"

All this made Ronnie feel very sad. If only he could do something really special, he thought, something to make all the other reindeer really proud of him...

Ronnie tried hard to think what he could do. But long after the other reindeer were asleep and night had fallen, he still hadn't thought of anything. He gave a big sigh, looking up at the sky.

Father Christmas was out on a practice sleigh-ride, ready for Christmas Eve. But Ronnie didn't know that. He was watching the reindeer flying! If they could fly, he told himself, he could, too!

Ronnie began practising the very next day. Off he went to the top of a hill. He took a deep breath, ran as fast as he could, then jumped, flapping his hooves about and hoping he would fly!

But flying wasn't nearly so easy as it looked! Ronnie just fell to the ground, squashing a clump of lovely, fresh grass! "Ronnie!" roared Stag. "You're getting into trouble AGAIN!"

Ronnie tried all sorts of things —
hopping about on each hoof,
jumping up and down... being
so busy and moving about so
much, he hardly noticed the
snow which had begun to fall...

And this time, before Ronnie
could make a jump, his back
hooves slid on the icy ground. Up
he went into the air, his legs
moving all at once. Ronnie could
hardly believe it!

When Ronnie landed in the soft snow, he could see that he was quite a long way from where he had jumped - and that could only mean one thing! "I CAN fly!" he cried. "I can FLY!"

It was so exciting, Ronnie didn't want to stop! Again and again, he tried sliding on the snow, then lifting up his hooves and sailing through the air! "Look at me!" he cried. "I'm FLYING!"

Some of the other reindeer had already seen him! Off they went to tell Stag and Mother Deer about Ronnie learning to fly! But someone else had seen Ronnie, too...

"Oh, no!" groaned Father Christmas. "That little reindeer down there is trying to fly! And I thought EVERYONE knew that only MY reindeer can fly across the sky!"

Just then, Ronnie took another
jump, flapped his legs and his
hooves about, and fell down –
THUMP!
Poor Ronnie! He could not help
grinding his teeth in pain!

"I must do something about this," Father Christmas decided. "Steady, my reindeer. Let me get a sprinkle of stardust!" Soon, he knew, Ronnie would try to fly yet again.

Sure enough, the little reindeer
ran over the snow. Then he lifted
his legs, tucked in his hooves,
and... WHOOSH! Up he flew into
the sky in a shower of magic
stardust!

With stars twinkling and the moon shining, Ronnie could see all the trees and bushes, now far, far below. A cool wind blew on his hooves and his legs until they didn't hurt at all.

"Oh," said Ronnie, "now I know how it REALLY feels to fly!"
"You had worked hard, trying to learn," said Father Christmas. "You deserved to have your Christmas wish come true."

By now, the other reindeer had
called Stag and Mother Deer.
"Ronnie? Flying?" roared Stag.
"Rubbish! Where is he?"
"If he's got into trouble," said
Mother Deer, "I'll —"

But none of them ever knew
what she would do. Because, at
that moment, the moon came
out from behind a cloud, making
all the deer look up into the
starry sky.

"It's Father Christmas!" breathed
the little reindeer.
"And his reindeer sleigh..." added
Stag, almost in a whisper.
"And RONNIE!" cried Mother
Deer. "He really CAN fly!"

Father Christmas guided his sleigh behind a mass of white, snowy cloud.

"Time for you to go, Ronnie!" he smiled. "This moonbeam will take you safely home."

Sliding down a moonbeam was
as much fun as flying. "Thank
you, Father Christmas!" cried
Ronnie. "I hope I see you again!"
"You will, Ronnie!" laughed
Father Christmas. "You will!"

Ronnie landed safely on all four hooves. Now Stag, Mother Deer and all the reindeer wanted to hear about how he had flown with Father Christmas across the starry skies!

And if he slid on the snow, or fell in the mud or trod in the water, nobody minded too much. They were all so proud to know such a clever, wonderful, splendid reindeer like Ronnie!

O LITTLE TOWN OF BETHLEHEM

O little town of Bethlehem,
How still we see thee lie;
Above thy deep and dreamless sleep
The silent stars go by.

Yet in thy dark streets shineth
The everlasting Light;
The hopes and fears of all the years
Are met in thee tonight.

GUESS WHO!

F is for the Fur trim
    round his big boots and hat,

A is for his Apple cheeks,
    so cuddly, round and fat!

T is for the Toys he brings, and

H his Happy smile!

E is for his Eyes, so bright, and –

R each Reindeer mile!

C is for the Chimney stack, and
H the Hearth below.
R for his Red cloak and hood,
I the Ice and snow!
S is for the Stockings,
T is for the Tree – and
M is for the Mistletoe,
which we all love to see!

A is for the Angels,
who on Christmas cards appear
S for dear old Santa Claus,
who visits us each year!

PERCY'S
HAPPY
CHRISTMAS

Illustrated by Stephen Holmes

There was once a little, plain plate
called Percy. He was round, shiny
and well-scrubbed, but he was not
very happy.

"Christmas is coming. The house is
full of beautiful things," Percy
sighed. "Why am I so plain?"

Percy told the teapot, "I wish I had
a pretty blue and gold pattern like
you. Or a picture on my tummy like
the baby's dish. Or holly leaves
like the Christmas paper plates.
Why am I so plain?"

"I wish I was beautiful," he said,
unhappily.
"Be thankful you're not chipped!"
snapped a cross saucer.
"Or scratched!" mumbled a tired,
old saucepan.

"Be thankful you're not faded!" sighed the cream jug, whose pattern had washed away...

"Or broken!" groaned a mug with no handle.

But Percy did not listen to them.

One cold and frosty morning, Bertie Bear, who lived in Percy's house, rushed into the kitchen, calling, "Mummy, which plate can I have? I promised to take one to school today."

"Take an old one, dear," said his mother. "Here, this plain, old one will do. I don't need it any more. It doesn't match any of my other nice things, anyway."

Percy was so upset he almost cracked. To think that the others should hear him called old and unwanted, just because his family had been lost in various accidents!

Then Percy found himself being wrapped in newspaper and thrust into Bertie's dark satchel with all the books and pencils. He sobbed all the way to school.

The pencils thought him very silly
and the books wouldn't speak to
him at all. Percy was very glad
when he was lifted out and put on
the teacher's desk.

"Oh, thank you, Bertie," said Miss
Frenshaw. "That's just right!"
Percy's spirits lifted...
"Just leave it there until after lunch,
and we'll see what we can do with
it, then."

Percy was puzzled. What would happen next? He sat very still, watching the children doing their sums. He had no idea, that later on that afternoon, he would be changed forever!

When they had finished their work,
the children gathered together fir-
cones, holly, glue, ribbons and gold
paint. They pasted and cut, painted
and coloured, until Percy was no
longer a plain plate at all!

They had painted a beautiful snow scene on his tummy with little snowflakes and fir trees. Sprigs of holly and bows circled his rim, and everyone thought he looked absolutely wonderful!

"There is no doubt he's our best Christmas decoration," said Miss Frenshaw. "He's not a plain plate now, he's a perfect plate! Let's put him in the window so everyone can see him."

How proud Percy was! His smile
was bigger than it had ever been.
He sat in the window with the
other decorations and thought
what a lucky, little plate he was.

The afternoon drew to a close and the children sang carols. As the music floated by him, Percy stared out of the window. Snow had begun to fall. What a wonderful Christmassy scene!

Soon parents arrived to take their children home. They could see Percy in the window as they walked through the snow, towards the school door.

Bertie rushed out to meet his mum
and couldn't wait to tell her all
about his exciting day! Before they
set off home, he turned around and
waved to Percy.

Percy waved back, but he wasn't sure if Bertie had noticed.

"I would never have recognised our old plate," said Bertie's mum. "He looks so beautiful, now."

It seemed quiet in the classroom when all the children had gone, but Percy was happy just to sit there and remember everything that had happened.

Now, Percy was happy, loved and beautiful. It had been a wonderful day. He couldn't wait for tomorrow, when the children would return and he would be able to sit and watch them play, once again.

CHRISTMAS IS COMING

Christmas is coming,
The goose is getting fat,
Please put a penny
In the old man's hat.
If you haven't got a penny,
A ha'penny will do;
If you haven't got a ha'penny,
Then God bless you!

Index

Index

Index

Index